MICHAEL DAHL PRESENTS
SUPER FUNNY
JOKE BOOKS

The

Funny
Farm

JOKES ABOUT
DOGS, CATS, DUCKS, SNAKES,
BEARS, AND OTHER ANIMALS

PICTURE WINDOW BOOKS
a capstone imprint

MICHAEL DAHL PRESENTS SUPER FUNNY JOKE BOOKS

are published by Picture Window Books
a Capstone Imprint
151 Good Counsel Drive, P.O. Box 669
Mankato, Minnesota 56002
www.capstonepub.com

Laughs on a Leash and *Zoodles* were previously published
by Picture Window Books, copyright © 2004
Giggle Bubbles, Roaring with Laughter, and *Sit! Stay! Laugh!*
were previously published by Picture Window Books, copyright © 2005

Library of Congress Cataloging-in-Publication data
is available on the Library of Congress website.
ISBN: 978-1-4048-5772-8 (library binding)
ISBN: 978-1-4048-6369-9 (paperback)

Art Director: **KAY FRASER**
Designer: **EMILY HARRIS**
Production Specialist: **JANE KLENK**

TABLE OF CONTENTS

GIGGLE BUBBLES:

UNDERWATER JOKES

Where do mummies like to swim?

In the Dead Sea.

What do killer whales eat for dinner?

Fish and ships.

What did one ocean say to the other ocean?

"Nice to sea you!"

How did the oyster
call his friends?

He used his shellphone.

What do you call a
baby whale?

A little squirt.

How can you tell the sailboat
is in love with the island?

It hugs the shore.

What's the difference between a piano and a fish?

You can tune a piano, but you can't tuna fish.

How much does it cost for a pirate to get his ears pierced?

A buccaneer.

What type of fish comes out at night?

A starfish.

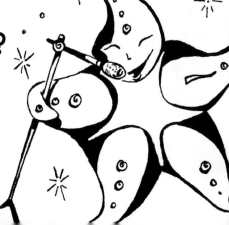

How can you tell if an octopus
parked in your driveway?

From the squid marks.

Why didn't the crab share his toys
with his little brother?

Because he was shellfish.

Why was the pirate so skinny?

Because he had a sunken chest.

Why was the mother octopus so upset?

All her kids needed new shoes.

How did the ocean explorer know he had discovered land?

He was shore of it.

WHAT DO YOU CALL A WHALE IN A BUS?

Why couldn't the sailor play cards?

Because the crew was sitting on the deck.

What do you do with a blue whale?

Try to cheer him up!

Why is a pirate ship a good place to buy stuff?

Because it has a big sail.

SALE

How can you tell the ocean is friendly?

It's always waving.

Why did the surfer fall asleep while riding the waves?

He was board silly.

What kind of sandwich does a shark eat?

Peanut butter and jellyfish.

What day do fish hate the most?

Fryday!

Why did the dolphin cross the ocean?

To get to the other tide.

Why are fish easy to weigh?

They come with their own scales.

What bus crossed the ocean?

Columbus.

What happens when you throw a blue rock into the Red Sea?

It gets wet!

How do you close an envelope underwater?

With a seal.

What types of little cars do fish like to race?

Go-carps!

What fish prowls in the jungle?

A tiger shark.

What sits on the bottom of the ocean and shivers?

A nervous wreck!

Where do pirates like to hang out?

At the ARRRRcade.

What do you call a seabird's date?

His gullfriend.

WHAT'S BEHIND A PIRATE'S PATCH?

HIS AYYYYYYYYYYY, MATEY!

What kind of ships
carry vampires?

Blood vessels.

What's the best day
to go to the beach?

Sunday.

What kind of hair does the
ocean have?

Wavy.

Why are fish so smart?

Because they live in schools.

Why is it impossible to starve on a desert island?

Because of all the sand which is there.

What do you get when you mix an electric eel with a squid?

A shocked-opus.

What kind of fish
likes to tell jokes?

Clownfish.

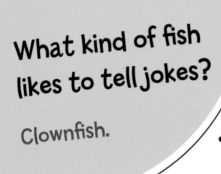

What kind of waves
wash up on the shore
of a tiny island?

Microwaves.

WHAT KIND OF FISH DO PIRATES HIDE IN TREASURE CHESTS?

GOLDFISH.

ROARING WITH LAUGHTER:

ANIMAL JOKES

What do you get when you put a turkey in the freezer?

A brrrrrrrrrd.

What do you get if you cross a bumblebee with a doorbell?

A humdinger!

Why did the snowman call his watchdog Frost?

Because Frost bites!

Why did the pelican get kicked out of the hotel?

It had a big bill.

Why did the bee trip over the flower?

It was a stumblebee.

What does a cow read in the morning?

The moospaper.

What do you get when you cross a duck with an alligator?

A quackodile.

Where did the cow go on the weekend?

To the mooovies.

How did the little fish get to school?

It took the octobus.

What kind of snake is good at cleaning cars?

A windshield viper.

What do you call a camel at the North Pole?

Lost!

What time is it when an elephant sits on a fence?

Time to fix the fence!

What do polar bears eat for lunch?

Icebergers.

What's big and gray and has lots of horns?

An elephant marching band.

WHAT KIND OF ANT IS GOOD AT MATH?

What do chickens do on Valentine's Day?

They give each other pecks.

What did one bee say to the other bee on a hot summer day?

"Sure is swarm, isn't it?"

What did the pony say when it had a sore throat?

"Sorry, but I'm a little horse."

What goes "zzub zzub"?

A bee flying backwards.

What is the biggest ant in the world?

An elephant.

What follows a lion wherever it goes?

Its tail.

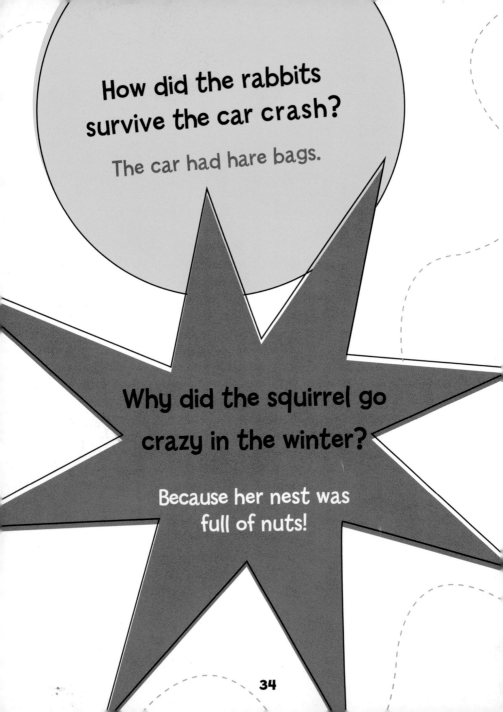

How did the rabbits survive the car crash?

The car had hare bags.

Why did the squirrel go crazy in the winter?

Because her nest was full of nuts!

What do you call a crate full of ducks?

A box of quackers.

Why did the mole dig a tunnel into the bank?

To burrow some money.

How do rich birds make their money?

They invest in the stork market.

Why do turkeys always lose at baseball?

They can only hit fowl balls.

What kind of lions live in your front yard?

Dandelions.

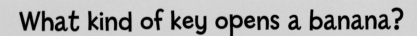

What kind of key opens a banana?

A monkey.

What did the little centipede say to his mother when they went shopping?

"I need a new pair of shoes.
And a new pair of shoes.
And a new pair of shoes . . ."

Why was the rooster all wet?

He was covered with cock-a-doodle dew.

What did the duck say when she bought some lipstick?

Put it on my bill.

WHAT DO YOU CALL A CHICKEN THAT LIKES TO EAT CEMENT?

What do you call a crazy chicken?

A cuckoo cluck.

How did the grizzly catch a cold?

He walked outside with just his bear feet.

What did the cow ride when her car broke down?

A mootorcycle.

What do chickens eat at birthday parties?

Coopcakes.

Where do cows go in a rocket ship?

To the moooooon.

What do rabbits use to make their ears look nice?

Hare spray.

What do bees
wear when they
go to work?

Buzzness suits.

When dolphins play football, how do
they know which team gets the ball?

They flip for it.

Why do mother kangaroos hate
rainy days?

Because the kids have to play inside.

What kind of airplane do elephants ride in?

Jumbo jets.

Why don't animals play cards in the jungle?

There are too many cheetahs.

Why do birds fly south in the winter?

It's too far to walk.

What is the best kind of computer bug to have?

A spider. They make the best websites.

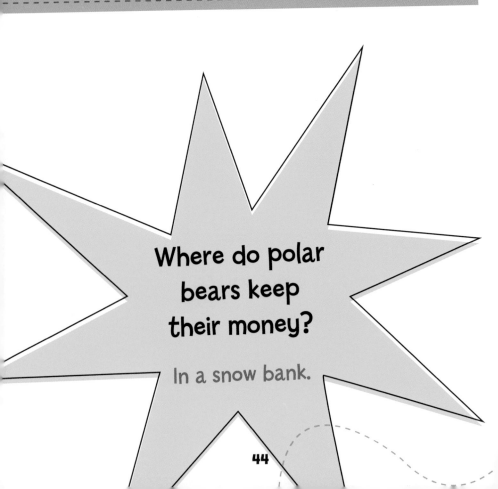

Where do polar bears keep their money?

In a snow bank.

How did the flea travel
from dog to dog?

It went itch-hiking.

Why did the crow perch on
the telephone wire?

He was going to make a
long-distance caw.

LAUGHS ON A LEASH:

PET JOKES

How can you tell if a snake
is a baby?

It has a rattle.

What did the dog
say when he sat
on sandpaper?

Ruff! Ruff!

Why did the little girl make her
pet chicken sit on the roof?

She liked egg rolls.

What kind of dog likes flowers?

A budhound.

Why do dogs have such big families?

Because they each have four paws.

What kind of dog wears a uniform and a badge?

A guard dog.

Why do baby skunks
make the worst pets?

They're always little stinkers.

What do you get when you put
a kitten in the copy machine?

A copycat.

Where do dogs go when they
lose their tails?

A retail store.

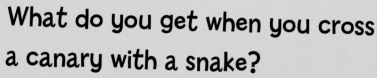

What do you get when you cross a canary with a snake?

A sing-a-long.

What pet comes with its own mobile home?

A turtle.

Why did the cowboy buy a dachshund?

Everybody told him to "get a long, little doggie."

What type of music do bunnies play at parties?

Hip-hop.

Why don't dogs make good dancers?

Because they have two left feet!

DID YOU HEAR ABOUT THE GOLDFISH WHO BECAME A QUARTERBACK?

HE WANTED TO PLAY
IN THE SUPER BOWL!

Why did the puppy bite the man's ankle?

Because it couldn't reach any higher.

What kind of coat does a pet dog wear?

A petticoat.

Why is a group of puppies called a litter?

Because they mess up the whole house.

What do you get if your cat drinks lemonade?

A sour puss.

Why did the cat buy a computer?

So he could play with a mouse of his very own.

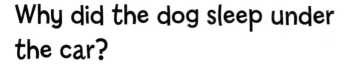

Why did the dog sleep under the car?

He wanted to wake up oily.

How do you spell "mousetrap" with just three letters?

C-A-T.

What do you call kittens that like to bowl?

Alley cats.

What do you call young dogs that play in the snow?

Slush puppies.

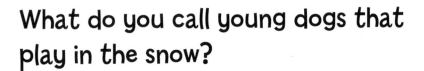

What did the hungry dalmatian say after a meal?

"That hit the spots!"

How many pet skunks do you have?

Quite a phew!

What do you give a pet rabbit for dessert?

A hopsicle.

What kind of dog can cook dinner for its owner?

An oven mutt.

What is a polygon?

When your pet parrot flies out of its cage.

Why did the kitten put the letter "M" into the freezer?

To turn some ice into mice.

What did the girl do when she found her pet dog eating the dictionary?

She took the words right out of his mouth.

What kind of dog is like a short skirt?

A peekin' knees.

What pet fish are the most expensive?

Goldfish.

Why did the boy take a bag of oats to bed?

To feed his nightmare.

What kinds of beds do fish sleep on?

Waterbeds.

What do you call a koala without any socks on?

Bearfoot.

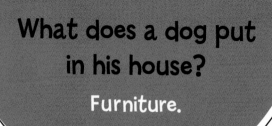

What does a dog put
in his house?

Furniture.

How did the girl talk
to her pet fish?

She dropped it a line.

How can you tell that carrots are
good for your eyes?

Because rabbits never wear glasses.

What do you give a dog with a fever?

Mustard. It's the best thing for a hot dog.

Why are some fish found at the bottom of the ocean?

Because they dropped out of school.

What do you get when you cross an elephant with a goldfish?

Swimming trunks.

What do frogs like to drink
in the winter?

Hot croako.

Why are mice so noisy after
they take a bath?

They're squeaky clean.

What do cats drink on hot summer days?

Miced tea.

Which side of a cat has the most fur?

The outside!

What did the dog say about his day in the woods?

"Bark, bark, bark, bark . . ."

WHAT DO DOGS LIKE TO EAT FOR BREAKFAST?

POOCHED EGGS.

What kind of pet can you stand on?

A carpet.

What do mice do when they're at home all day?

Mousework.

What's the best time to
buy a pet canary?

When it's going cheep!

CHEEP!

What kind of pet
can tell time?

A watchdog.

Mom: Why is your pet bunny
so unhappy?

Emily: It's having a bad hare day.

Why can't dalmatians hide from their owners?

They're always spotted.

Why did the girl oil her pet mouse?

It squeaked.

Police officer: Young man! What is your dog doing in the street?

Boy: About seven miles an hour.

How do rabbits play the piano?

They play by ear.

Why is an octopus such a sweet pet?

It's covered with suckers.

How does a rabbit feel if it breaks a leg?

Unhoppy.

What type of pet makes big holes in the street?

Roadents.

What kind of pet can help you read?

An alphapet.

Jenny: My cat is lost!

Dad: Put up a poster.

Jenny: Why? My cat can't read.

Bob: Have you ever seen a fishbowl?

Jay: No. How do they get their fins into those holes in the ball?

ZOODLES:
ANIMAL RIDDLES

What side of a chicken has the most feathers?

The outside.

What do chimpanzees eat for a snack?

Chocolate chimp cookies.

What kind of pigs do you find on the highway?

Road hogs.

How can you tell when it's raining cats and dogs?

When you step into a poodle.

What do you call a crab that plays baseball?

A pinch hitter.

Where do sheep go for haircuts?

The BAA-BAA shop.

What kind of dog has no tail,
no nose, and no fur?

A hot dog.

What happened when the bee
telephoned his friend?

He got a buzzy signal.

What do you call a hot and noisy duck?

A firequacker.

What animal talks the most?

A yak.

What school contest did the skunk win?

The smelling bee.

What pet makes the loudest noise?

A trumpet.

What kind of vitamins do fish need?

Vitamin sea.

What do you call the top of a dog house?

The woof.

Who steals soap from the bathroom?

The robber duckie.

WHAT DID THE BANANA DO WHEN IT SAW THE HUNGRY MONKEY?

NOTHING. THE BANANA SPLIT.

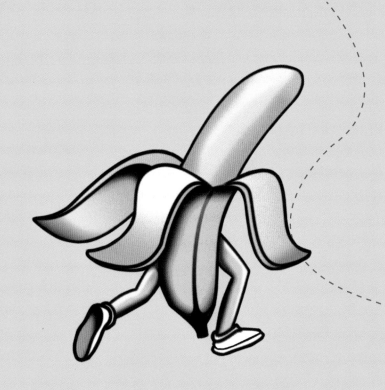

HOW TO BE FUNNY

The following tips will help you become rich, famous, and popular. Well, maybe not. However, they will help you tell a good joke.

WHAT TO DO:

- Know the joke.
- Allow suspense to build, but don't drag it out too long.
- Make the punch line clear.
- Be confident, use emotion, and smile.

WHAT NOT TO DO:

- Do not ask your friend over and over if they "get it."
- Do not speak in a different language than your audience.
- Do not tell the same joke every day.
- Do not keep saying, "This joke is so funny!"